Cooperation

STONE SOUP

Adapted by Mary Rowitz
Illustrated by Sharron O'Neil

Copyright © 2005 Publications International, Ltd.
All rights reserved.

This publication may not be reproduced in whole or in part by any means whatsoever without written permission from

Louis Weber, C.E.O., Publications International, Ltd., 7373 North Cicero Avenue, Lincolnwood, Illinois 60712

Ground Floor, 59 Gloucester Place, London W1U 8JJ

www.pilbooks.com

Permission is never granted for commercial purposes.

8 7 6 5 4 3 2 1

ISBN 1-4127-3757-5

A hungry traveler had been roaming the countryside for a long time, and he had not eaten a good meal in quite a while. One day the traveler spotted a lovely village off in the distance. He became very excited and said to himself, "I'm bound to find someone in the village who will share a meal with me."

As the traveler hurried to the town, he tripped over a stone in the road. The stone was not like any that the traveler had ever seen before. It was perfectly smooth and oval in shape. The traveler looked at the stone carefully and decided he would keep it. "You never know when a stone like this might come in handy," he said.

Then he happily headed to the village. His empty stomach grumbled as he walked.

When the traveler arrived, things did not go as well as he had hoped. He stopped at a few houses, but no one had any food to share.

One house the traveler came to was very quiet. All the doors and windows were closed, and the shades were drawn. The traveler began to think that no one was home. Finally a maid appeared in the doorway.

"Can you spare some food?" the traveler asked her. "I have been traveling for days, and I am very hungry."

"I'm sorry, but I have only a few potatoes," the maid said. "There's not enough to spare or share. Why don't you try my neighbor next door?"

"I already have," said the traveler, "but he was very grumpy and just slammed the door. It looks like finding some food in this village will be more difficult than I thought." Still the hungry traveler refused to give up.

The traveler visited every house in the village, but no one had enough food to spare or share. At one house there was only cabbage, the next had only carrots, and a third had only salt and pepper.

Since there was no food for the hungry traveler, he decided to move on. Before he got very far, he began to feel tired. He decided to get some rest in the cool shade of a tree just outside the village. As he sat under the tree, the traveler looked back at the quiet little town. "It's a shame," he thought, "such a nice village and such a beautiful day, but nobody is outdoors visiting."

Then the traveler reached into his bag and took out the smooth, oval stone that he had found earlier in the day. As he sat admiring the stone, the traveler suddenly had a brilliant idea!

The traveler ran back to the village and shouted, "Come out of your houses, everybody! I have a magic stone, and it will give us enough food for a wonderful meal. Everyone in town will have plenty to eat, and there will even be enough to spare and share!" One by one, the curious villagers peeked out of their doors and windows.

The grumpy villager who had earlier slammed the door on the traveler looked out of his window and shouted, "What's all the racket about?"

"Come help me make a pot of delicious stone soup," said the traveler.

The maid stepped out of her house as two excited children ran up to the traveler. "Is that your stomach I hear growling?" one child asked.

"Yes," the other replied, "I am very hungry."

"Does anybody have a large soup kettle to get us started?" the traveler asked.

"I've got one that you can use," said the big, grumpy villager, "but I don't think it will do any good. I don't think your magic stone will really work."

"I guess we'll find out soon enough," said one lady. "I certainly hope he can make soup out of a stone. I haven't had good soup in a long time."

The grumpy villager brought out his large kettle, filled it with water, and placed it on a pile of sticks for the fire. "Now let's see if that magic stone of yours can really make enough soup for all of us," he said.

"Don't worry," said the traveler. "There will be plenty."

The traveler placed the smooth, oval stone into the kettle of water and began to stir. After a little while he tasted the soup. "Not bad," the traveler said, "but I think it could use some salt and pepper and perhaps a potato."

"I've got salt and pepper," said one of the young ladies. "I'll run home and get it."

The maid added her potatoes, and once again the traveler stirred the soup. When he tasted it again, all the villagers watched him with anticipation.

"This is very good, but it would taste even better with some carrots and cabbage," said the traveler. Then a young boy ran home to get some carrots, and a little girl ran home to get her cabbage.

By now, everyone was having so much fun. Even the big, grumpy villager was no longer grumpy. "Let's make this meal a party!" he shouted.

Finally the traveler announced that the stone soup was ready. He filled all the bowls, and the villagers began to eat. Afterward there was plenty of soup left over. "There's enough to spare and share!" said the young lady.

The villagers were so happy after dinner that they did not want the evening to end. They started playing music together and dancing with one another. At last the village was alive with chatter and laughter.

"I didn't know you could play the banjo," the maid said to the big villager.

"And I didn't know you could play the washboard," he responded.

"I think there was a lot we didn't know until the traveler came along," said the maid.

The next morning, the traveler said good-bye to his new friends in the village. It was time for him to leave and travel somewhere new. "I want you to have this," the traveler said as he handed the smooth, oval stone to the villagers. "Now you will always be able to make stone soup together, and you will never be hungry or sad or grumpy again."

Each of the villagers hugged the traveler. "Come back and visit us again," said the maid.

"You are always welcome," said the big villager. They were all very grateful, and they all hoped to see the kind traveler again.

As the traveler headed out of the little village, he stumbled over another stone in the road. He picked it up at once and admired its jagged edges. The traveler looked at the stone carefully and finally decided to keep it. "You never know when a stone like this might come in handy," he said to himself as he placed it in his bag.

Cooperation

Cooperation means working with others to get things done. The hungry traveler used the stone to show the villagers how to cooperate. When the traveler came to town, each villager had a little bit of food but not enough for an entire meal. The traveler helped the villagers work together to make a delicious soup. When they cooperated, the villagers found they had plenty of food for everyone.

Cooperation can make difficult things easy, and it can also be lots of fun. The villagers learned that it is easy to make friends when you work together.